To my parents,
Greg and Ursula—M.J.

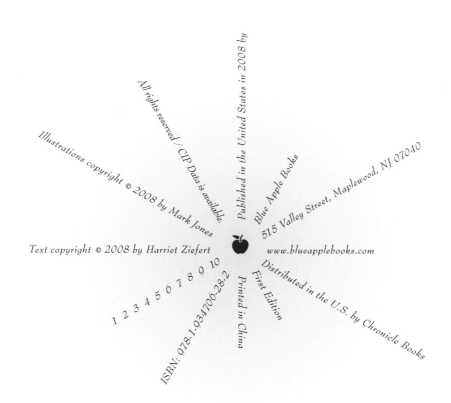

Published in the United States in 2008 by

Blue Apple Books

515 Valley Street, Maplewood, NJ 07040

www.blueapplebooks.com

Distributed in the U.S. by Chronicle Books

First Edition

Printed in China

Illustrations copyright © 2008 by Mark Jones

Text copyright © 2008 by Harriet Ziefert

1 2 3 4 5 6 7 8 9 10

ISBN: 978-1-934706-28-2

For Charlie—H.Z.

SNOW PARTY

by Harriet Ziefert   *illustrated by* Mark Jones

Blue Apple Books

The snow had been falling quietly all night long.

By morning a thick blanket
of white covered the countryside.

It seemed as if nothing existed in the world but beautiful snow.

Suddenly, as if by magic,

snow women . . .

snow men . . .

and snow children
began to appear.

Some carried bags; some carried boxes.

"Here is a perfect spot!" said a snow woman.

The snow people began to work,
stringing lights, setting up tables,
and unpacking bags.

"You'll see soon,"
said his mother.

"What's in the box?"
a boy in a red cap asked.

"Sweeping the pond is hard,"
said a boy with a broom.

"Right," said his friend.
"But tonight is going to be so much fun.
We're going to have a special party."

The musicians,
carrying all kinds
of instruments,
arrived in the late
afternoon.

Everything was almost ready.

The lights twinkled,
the tables were set,
the food was prepared,
and the dance floor was ready.

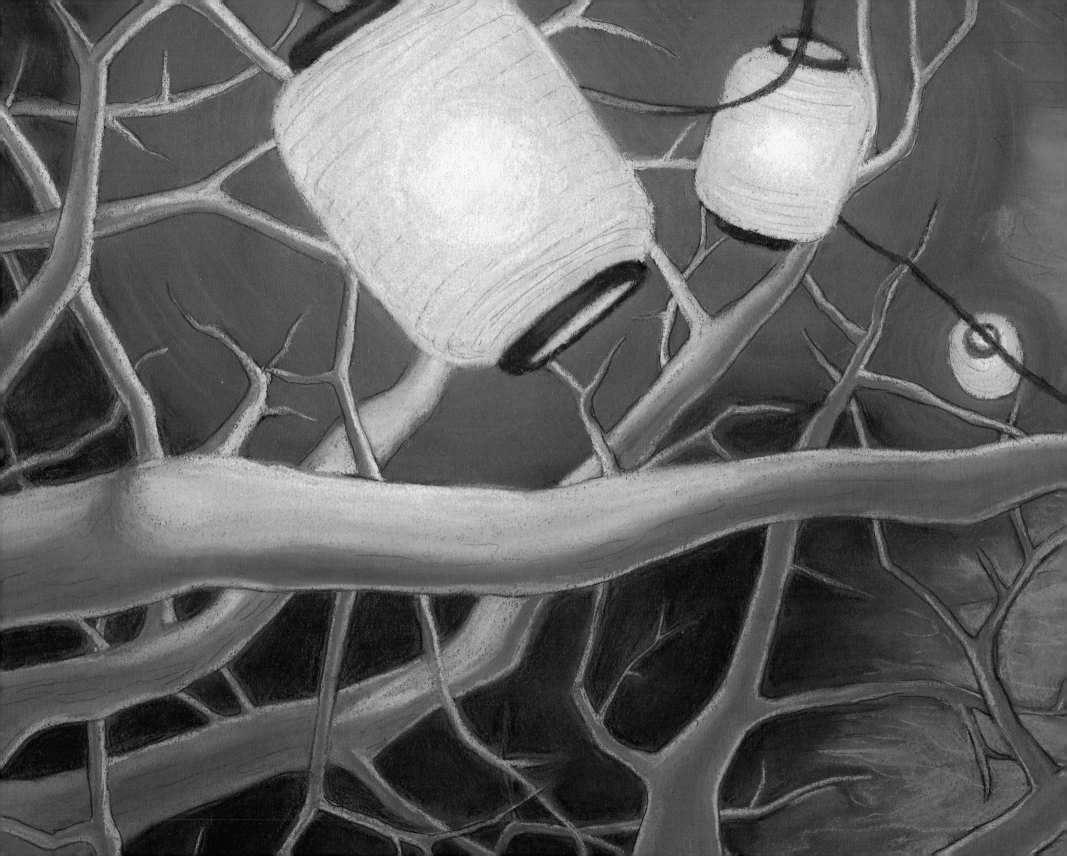

"Today is the shortest day of the year," said a snowman wearing a top hat.

"This is when we celebrate the winter solstice,
the first day of winter. And when the first snow
of the year falls on the first day of winter, we have a snow party!"
Everybody clapped and cheered.
Hooray for winter! Hooray for snow!

The snow people ate . . .

and danced . . .

When the box was unwrapped,
snow-white butterflies emerged.
They circled round and round
the joyful snow people.

And then snow began to fall—
very quietly.

The snow fell and fell . . .

It was still falling as the partygoers
packed up their belongings and went on their way.

By morning, a new blanket of white covered the countryside.
It was as if the snow people had never been there.

But some of us know better.